for Violet upstairs

Library of Congress Cataloging-in-Publication Data:
Names: Watkins, Rowboat, 1967- author.
Title: Most marshmallows / Rowboat Watkins.
Description: San Francisco, California : Chronicle Books LLC, [2018] |
Summary: Most marshmallows like to watch television and lead normal lives—
but some marshmallows dream of greater things.
Identifiers: LCCN 2017045067 | ISBN 9781452159591 (alk. paper)
Subjects: LCSH: Marshmallow—Juvenile fiction. | Conduct of life—Juvenile fiction.
| Dreams—Juvenile fiction. | CYAC: Marshmallow—Fiction. | Conduct of life—Fiction. | Dreams—Fiction.
Classification: LCC PZ7.1.W4 Mo 2018 | DDC [E]—dc23 LC record available
at https://lccn.loc.gov/2017045067

ISBN 978-1-4521-5959-1
Manufactured in China.

MIX
Paper from
responsible sources
FSC™ C008047

Design by Sara Gillingham Studio.
Typeset in Futuramano and hand-lettered by the artist.
The pictures were built out of marshmallows, construction paper, cake sprinkles,
cardboard, acorn tops, twisty ties, pencil, and whatever else was needed.

10 9 8 7 6 5 4 3 2

Chronicle Books LLC
680 Second Street
San Francisco, California 94107

Chronicle Books—we see things differently.
Become part of our community at www.chroniclekids.com.

MOST MARSHMALLOWS

Rowboat Watkins

chronicle books · san francisco

Most marshmallows   don't grow on trees

or come from storks

or even Mars.

Most marshmallows are mostly born

to one sweet parent or two

and live in homes

of one kind or another.

They celebrate birthdays.

They watch TV.

They go to school

most mornings

and learn to be squishy

and how to stand in rows

and why they can't breathe fire.

Most marshmallows eat dinner together

and fall asleep most nights

to dream about nothing.

But some marshmallows

somehow secretly know

that all marshmallows

can do anything

or be anything

they dare to imagine.

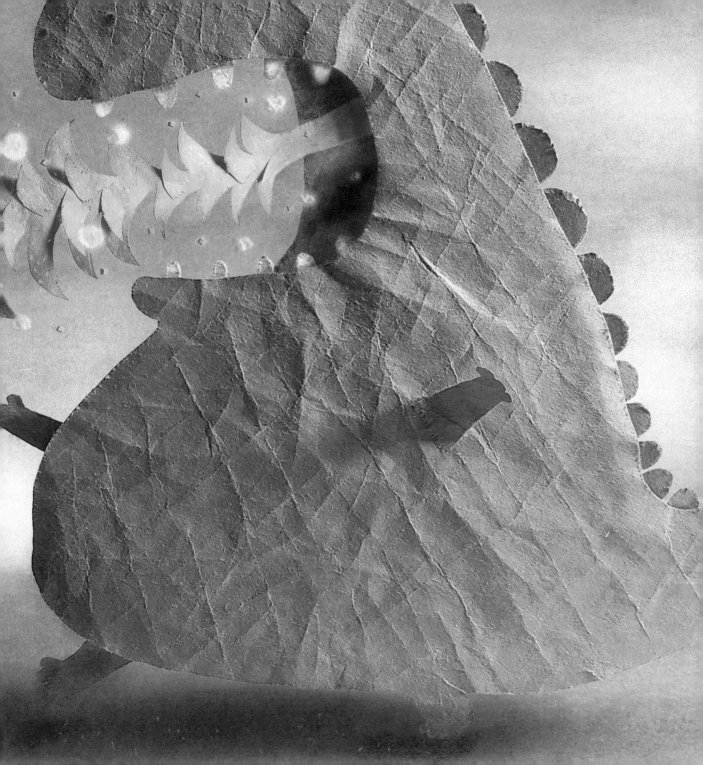

So **ROAR!**

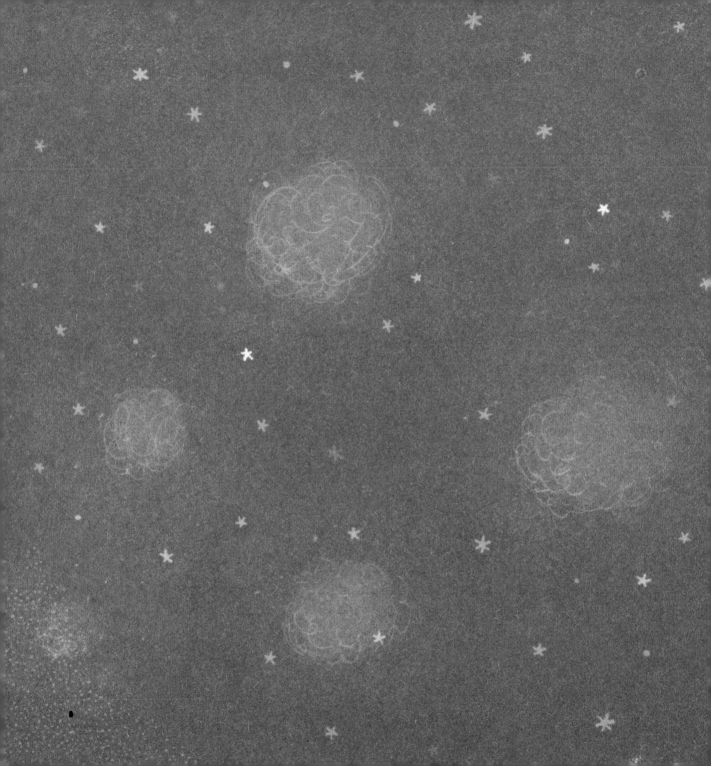